The New Friend

For Frances Schwartz,
once again
— C. Z.

The New Friend
Text copyright © 1968 by Charlotte Zolotow
Illustration copyright © 2021 by Benjamin Chaud
The original edition of The New Friend was published by Crowell, in 1968.

© Charlotte Zolotow Trust
This edition is published by arrangement with
Edite Kroll Literary Agency Inc, Saco, ME, USA
in conjunction with its duly appointed agent
Marotte et compagnie, agence littéraire, Paris, France.
All right reserved.

Editorial and art direction by Nadine Robert
Jacket design by Jolin Masson
Typeset: Galaxie Copernicus

The artwork for this book was created with watercolor, gouache, and pencil.

Library and Archives Canada Cataloguing in Publication
Title: The new friend / Charlotte Zolotow ; illustrations, Benjamin Chaud.
Names: Zolotow, Charlotte, 1915-2013, author. | Chaud, Benjamin, illustrator.
Identifiers: Canadiana 20210042443 | ISBN 9781990252013 (hardcover)
Classification: LCC PS3576.O45 N49 2021 | DDC j813/.54—dc23

ISBN 978-1-990252-01-3

Printed and bound in China

Milky Way Picture Books
38 Sainte-Anne Street
Varennes, QC J3X 1R5
Canada

www.milkywaypicturebooks.com

Charlotte Zolotow

The New Friend

art by Benjamin Chaud

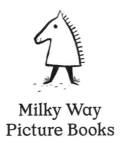

Milky Way
Picture Books

I had a friend
a dear friend
with long brown hair.

We walked together in the woods
and picked wildflowers

and waded in the brook
and touched the glistening stones
and then came home.

When it rained
we listened in the attic.

When it cleared
we went barefoot
in the wet grass.

When we were hungry
we had apples in the tree
and ate apple seeds
and talked together
while we ate.

We joked and jumped rope
and strung beads
and read books together
me and my friend.

One day I called for her
but she wasn't there.

I walked in the woods looking for her
and I found her with a different friend.
They picked wildflowers

and waded in the brook
and touched the glistening stones
and then went home.

I followed and saw them
jump rope and joke together
and sing the songs we had sung.

I went home
and I cried.
I cried all day
and cried myself to sleep.

I dreamed I found a new friend

who walked with me in the woods.

She showed me new paths
with flowers I had never seen.

And I woke up.

I will look for that new friend
and when I find her

I'll remember my first friend
my dear friend
with long brown hair.

But maybe then
I won't care!